Scientists who Changed the World

Stephen Hawking

Anita Croy

CRABTREE
PUBLISHING COMPANY
WWW.CRABTREEBOOKS.COM

CRABTREE
PUBLISHING COMPANY
WWW.CRABTREEBOOKS.COM

Author: Anita Croy
Editors: Sarah Eason, Melissa Boyd, Ellen Rodger
Proofreader and indexer: Jennifer Sanderson
Proofreader: Wendy Scavuzzo
Editorial director: Kathy Middleton
Design: Paul Myerscough and Lynne Lennon
Photo research: Rachel Blount
Print coordinator: Katherine Berti

Written, developed, and produced by Calcium

Photo Credits:
t=Top, c=Center, b=Bottom, l= Left, r=Right

Inside: NASA: Johns Hopkins University Applied Physics Laboratory/Southwest Research Institute: p. 20; JPL-Caltech/ESA/Harvard-Smithsonian CfA: p. 17t; Shutterstock: 3000ad: p. 46; Andrey_l: p. 59; Arindambanerjee: p. 55; Asetta: p. 21r; Bedrin: p. 58b; Castleski: p. 21b; Catwalker: p. 17b; Marusya Chaika: p. 7b; Andrea Danti: p. 18; Diyana Dimitrova: p. 6; E71lena: p. 47; Ron Ellis: p. 32; Juergen Faelchle: p. 41; FILINdesign: pp. 14tr, 15tl; Hayk_Shalunts: p. 50; Kathy Hutchins: p. 51; David Ionut: p. 9b; Georgios Kollidas: p. 7t; Koya979: p. 40; Liseykina: p. 29; Mopic: p. 16; NASA images: p. 12; Jurik Peter: p. 52; Phonlamai Photo: p. 49; Rungrote: p. 9r; Serato: p. 8; Umberto Shtanzman: p. 26; Ivan Smuk: p. 10; Spatuletail: p. 34; Twocoms: p. 4; Vchal: p. 25; Vector FX: p. 30bl; Marc Ward: p. 22; Wondervendy: p. 35t; Zita: p. 54; Wikimedia Commons: p. 14; Maximilien Brice, CERN: p. 38; Jim Campbell/Aero-News Network: p. 45; D-Wave Systems, Inc: p. 31; Biswarup Ganguly: p. 24; J-heavy: p. 30c; Ute Kraus, Physics education group Kraus, Universität Hildesheim, Space Time Travel, (background image of the milky way: Axel Mellinger): p. 37; AB Lagrelius & Westphal: p. 58t; NASA: p. 19; NASA/Paul E. Alers: pp. 36, 48; NASA/ESA: p. 28; NASA, ESA, M.J. Jee and H. Ford (Johns Hopkins University): p. 61; NASA/JPL-Caltech/ESA/CXC/STScI: p. 60; NASA/MSFC/David Higginbotham/Emmett Given: p. 56; NASA/WMAP Science Team: p. 27; Pacific & Atlantic Photos, Inc: p. 11; Hartmann Schedel: p. 15cr; Science Museum London/Science and Society Picture Library: p. 35c; Pete Souza: p. 42; SpaceX: p. 57; Lucas Taylor/CERN: p. 39.

Library and Archives Canada Cataloguing in Publication

Title: Stephen Hawking / Anita Croy.
Names: Croy, Anita, author.
Description: Series statement: Scientists who changed the world | Includes index.
Identifiers: Canadiana (print) 20200226215 |
  Canadiana (ebook) 2020022624X |
  ISBN 9780778782223 (hardcover) |
  ISBN 9780778782285 (softcover) |
  ISBN 9781427126146 (HTML)
Subjects: LCSH: Hawking, Stephen, 1942-2018—Juvenile literature.
  | LCSH: Physicists—Biography— Juvenile literature. |
  LCGFT: Biographies.
Classification: LCC QC16.H39 C76 2021 | DDC j530.092—dc23

Library of Congress Cataloging-in-Publication Data

Names: Croy, Anita, author.
Title: Stephen Hawking / Anita Croy.
Description: New York : Crabtree Publishing Company, [2021] |
  Series: Scientists who changed the world | Includes bibliographical references and index.
Identifiers: LCCN 2020017169 (print) |
  LCCN 2020017170 (ebook) |
  ISBN 9780778782223 (hardcover) |
  ISBN 9780778782285 (paperback) |
  ISBN 9781427126146 (ebook)
Subjects: LCSH: Hawking, Stephen, 1942-2018--Juvenile literature.
  | Physicists--Great Britain--Biography--Juvenile literature.
Classification: LCC QC16.H33 C76 2021 (print) |
  LCC QC16.H33 (ebook) | DDC 530.092 [B]--dc23
LC record available at https://lccn.loc.gov/2020017169
LC ebook record available at https://lccn.loc.gov/2020017170

Crabtree Publishing Company
www.crabtreebooks.com   1-800-387-7650

Printed in the U.S.A./082020/CG20200601

Copyright © **2021 CRABTREE PUBLISHING COMPANY.** All rights reserved. No part of this publication may be reproduced, stored in a retrieval system or be transmitted in any form or by any means, electronic, mechanical, photocopying, recording, or otherwise, without the prior written permission of Crabtree Publishing Company.

Published in Canada
Crabtree Publishing
616 Welland Ave.
St. Catharines, Ontario
L2M 5V6

Published in the United States
Crabtree Publishing
347 Fifth Ave
Suite 1402-145
New York, NY 10016

Published in the United Kingdom
Crabtree Publishing
Maritime House
Basin Road North, Hove
BN41 1WR

Published in Australia
Crabtree Publishing
3 Charles Street
Coburg North
VIC, 3058

Contents

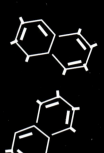

CHAPTER 1
STEPHEN HAWKING
Biography 4

CHAPTER 2
THE UNIVERSE
Background 12

CHAPTER 3
STUDYING SPACE
Breakthrough 22

CHAPTER 4
A BRIEF HISTORY OF TIME
Spreading Ideas 32

CHAPTER 5
INTERNATIONAL PROFILE
Reputation 42

CHAPTER 6
PUSHING KNOWLEDGE
Legacy 52

Glossary 62

For More Information 63

Index 64

CHAPTER 1

This photograph of Stephen Hawking was taken in 2015. It shows the sensor that monitored muscle movements in his cheek so he could speak through a computer.

STEPHEN HAWKING
Biography

Date of birth: January 8, 1942

Place of birth: Oxford, England

Mother: Isobel Eileen Walker Hawking

Father: Frank Hawking

Famous for: Being a cosmologist, or a scientist who studies the universe. He wrote *A Brief History of Time*. This bestseller explains the origins of the universe for non-scientists.

How he changed the world: Hawking's discoveries included the idea that **black holes** give off radiation, or energy, and can eventually shrink and vanish. He was the first to explain the universe's origins using **quantum physics**. This describes how the universe works at a level smaller than tiny **atoms** and **particles**. He combined it with Albert Einstein's General **Theory of Relativity**. It explains how **gravity**, space, and time are related.

Hawking said that his GOAL was simple. He wanted a complete UNDERSTANDING of the UNIVERSE, why it is the way it is—and WHY it exists at all.

S. Hawking

A SMART HOUSEHOLD

Stephen Hawking was born in Oxford, England, on January 8, 1942. This was the 300th anniversary of when Galileo Galilei (1564–1642), the father of modern science, had died. Hawking would become one of the most famous scientists since Galileo.

Hawking's parents were graduates of the University of Oxford. Frank Hawking had studied medicine, and then became an epidemiologist, or a person who studies diseases. Isobel Hawking had been to Oxford in the 1930s to study philosophy, politics, and economics. Women had only been allowed to study at the university from the 1920s. Even with her degree, Isobel found it hard to find an academic job because she was a woman. She ended up working as a medical secretary, which is how she met Frank.

The Hawking family did not have a cat or dog. Instead, they kept bees in a hive in the basement to provide honey.

It was quite usual for the family to eat in silence because everyone was reading a book.

Stephen Hawking had two younger sisters, Mary and Philippa, and when he was 14 his parents adopted his younger brother, Edward. When Stephen was eight, the family moved to a town called St. Albans, north of London, where Frank had a new job. Their house was full of books. It was normal for the family to eat in silence because everyone was reading a book.

Ideas that changed the world

*Hawking once said that he was never top of his class at school, but that his classmates obviously saw that he had **potential** because they nicknamed him "Einstein."*

Exploring the ideas

Like other famous scientists, such as Sir Isaac Newton (1642–1727) and Albert Einstein (1879–1955), Stephen Hawking found his school lessons boring. None of these men excelled at school, and their grades were often average, even at university. However, all of them had a streak of genius that their classmates and teachers could easily identify. As well as finding school boring, Stephen missed a lot of school through sickness. His dad was frustrated with Stephen's attitude toward school. He really wanted Stephen to become a physician like himself.

Isaac Newton figured out three laws that explained motion.

HISTORY'S STORY

The one subject Hawking really enjoyed at school was math. His teacher, Dikran Tahta, encouraged him to study math at university. Hawking loved the endless possibilities that math problems gave and the satisfaction of solving them. He always credited Tahta with showing him how great math could be, and inspiring him to become a math professor.

A LAZY STUDENT

Stephen Hawking's school days were a story of not working very hard. This was probably because he was not challenged enough to take his work seriously. For almost his entire education, he did the minimum amount of work he needed to do to get by. Lucky for him, he did well enough to win scholarships.

Stephen attended middle and high school at St. Albans School. When he started in 1952, aged 10 and a year younger than his classmates, the school was already more than 1,000 years old. Stephen's teachers could tell he was smart, but his grades did not show it and he was near the bottom of his class. Stephen still enjoyed school. He hung out with his friends, played board games, made model aircraft, built his own fireworks, and did other things a normal kid would do. One of the things he most enjoyed was taking devices apart and putting them back together just to see how they worked.

Hawking enjoyed making model aircraft from plastic pieces provided in kits.

In 1958, as Stephen was finishing his high school early, he got interested in building new machines from scratch. Helped by his inspirational math teacher, Dikran Tahta, he and some friends built their own computer from spare parts. They called it the Logical Uniselector Computing Engine, or LUCE (Lucy) for short.

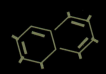

Oxford bound

Stephen's health was not good, so he often missed school because he was not feeling well. At this point, nobody realized that there was actually something seriously wrong. Despite his absences, he was smart enough to keep up.

Stephen wanted to follow in his parents' footsteps and attend Oxford University, which along with Cambridge, was the leading university in England. He did not want to study medicine like his dad, he wanted to study math. His school grades were average but, to get into Oxford, they needed to be excellent. Everyone advised him to wait until he was 18 to apply, but he was determined to take the entrance exam a year early. For once, he studied hard, and got an almost perfect score on the physics part of the exam. At his interview, Stephen's sense of humor and charm won over the interviewer and he was offered a scholarship to study physics.

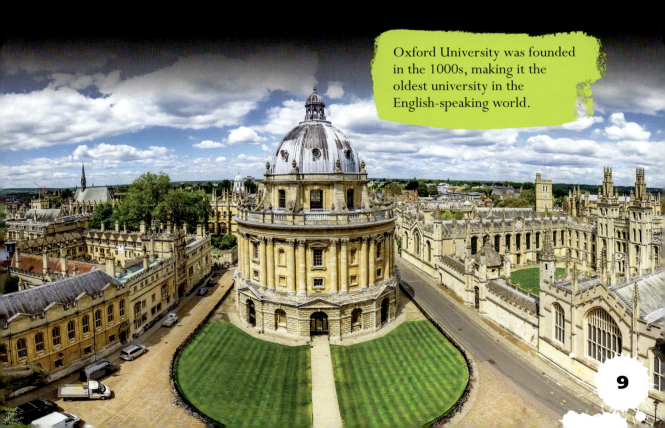

Oxford University was founded in the 1000s, making it the oldest university in the English-speaking world.

UNIVERSITY DAYS

In 1959, Stephen started at University College, Oxford, as one of three physics undergraduates. He chose physics, because at the time math was not a degree option at his college. Most of the other students were older than he was. Since serving in the military was then compulsory for young men, most of them had just quit the military and seemed much more mature. Still a teenager, Stephen struggled to fit in.

The physics course was three years long, and Stephen knew that he would only have to take examinations at the end of his final year. As a result, he did almost no work. He spent the first year reading science fiction novels. He grew his hair long and skipped classes because he found them too easy. To get over his shyness, he took up rowing. Not a natural sportsman, he was chosen as the cox, which meant sitting at the back of the boat and shouting instructions at the rowers!

In his final examinations, Stephen decided to answer only the **theoretical physics** questions he could figure out, and none of the questions that required revision to learn the answer. Theoretical physics uses math to explain the behavior of things that cannot be seen or measured, such as the tiny particles whizzing around inside atoms.

Hawking's role as cox meant that he steered the boat as the crew rowed.

Pass or fail

In Stephen's interview after the written exams, which were given to decide if he would graduate, his interviewers asked him why he should get a good mark. Stephen was worried that his professors thought he was lazy and difficult. He told them that, if they gave him a low mark, he would stay at Oxford—but if he got a high mark, he would go to graduate school in Cambridge. The examiners passed him, with flying colors!

Heading to Cambridge University

In fall 1962, Stephen arrived at Cambridge to study for a doctor of philosophy (PhD), or higher degree, in cosmology. He hoped his supervisor would be Professor Fred Hoyle (1915–2001), the most famous **astronomer** of the day. However, Hoyle was too busy to take on students, so Stephen was assigned to Dennis Sciama (1926–1999), a professor of cosmology. He was disappointed, but not for long. Sciama was one of the founders of modern cosmology.

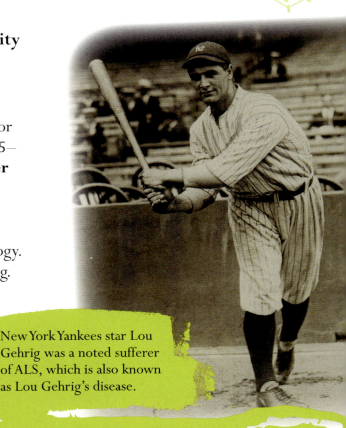

New York Yankees star Lou Gehrig was a noted sufferer of ALS, which is also known as Lou Gehrig's disease.

HISTORY'S STORY

While he was at Cambridge, Hawking noticed that his health was getting worse. He kept falling over and was having trouble with his speech. Tests showed that he was suffering from a form of **motor neuron disease** called amyotrophic lateral sclerosis (ALS). It attacks the nerves that connect the brain to muscles. ALS weakens the body, shortening a person's life.

CHAPTER 2

Distant clouds in the universe are nurseries where stars form from dust.

THE UNIVERSE
Background

At the start of Hawking's career, these were the key ideas that most, but not all, cosmologists held about the universe:

- The universe had started with a **Big Bang** explosion.
- The universe had grown from a tiny point and was still expanding.
- The universe was home to black holes, or areas of space with immensely strong gravity.
- Gravity and time were different, but related to each other.
- Stars were formed by gas clouds clumping together because of gravity.
- The universe was billions of years old.

Hawking said that the whole history of SCIENCE has been scientists' gradual realization that EVENTS do not happen in a RANDOM manner, but reflect an underlying ORDER. That order MAY or MAY NOT have been created by a GOD.

NEWTON AND EINSTEIN

When Stephen was a young man, physics was dominated by the ideas of two men. One was the English scientist Sir Isaac Newton, whose **theory** of gravity and three Laws of Motion made cosmology possible. The other was the German-American Albert Einstein, who came up with the General Theory of Relativity. Einstein suggested that black holes existed and that space was bent by gravity. However, no one had proven these ideas.

Sir Isaac Newton's ideas formed the basis of classical physics, which is how physicists examine the universe that can be seen with the human eye. Newton said that everything in the universe was held together by gravity, which pulls planets into orbits around stars.

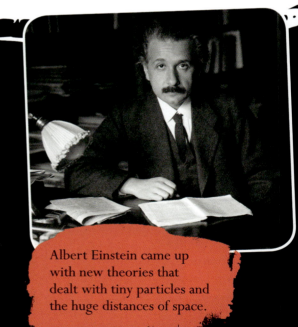

Albert Einstein came up with new theories that dealt with tiny particles and the huge distances of space.

Two hundred years later, Einstein's Theory of Relativity described the large-scale structure of the universe and the behavior of particles smaller than atoms. These subatomic particles were the building blocks of the universe. Einstein combined this new branch of physics—quantum physics—with his ideas about gravity. He argued that space and time were linked as space-time. Gravity could bend space-time. He believed that some points in space, now called black holes, would have such immense gravity that nothing would be able to resist their pull.

Ideas that changed the world

*Hawking said that, in just a few hundred years, humans have found a new way to think of ourselves. From believing Earth sits at the center of the universe, we have found that it orbits an average-sized star that is one of millions in our **galaxy**.*

Exploring the ideas

In the **Middle Ages**, the Church taught that God had created a universe with Earth at the center. The Sun and all the other planets orbited Earth. In the 1600s, when the Italian astronomer Galileo Galilei confirmed the theory of the Polish monk Nicolaus Copernicus (1473–1543) that Earth orbited the Sun, the Church punished Galileo. Since then, it has been proven that the Sun is at the center of our solar system and that our solar system is one of billions in the universe. Science keeps proving that our planet is far less significant than our **ancestors** believed.

This **medieval** illustration shows Earth at the center of the universe, while the Sun, moon, and planets revolve around it.

HISTORY'S STORY

A professor at Cambridge University, Sir Fred Hoyle discovered that the universe was much older than previously thought. He figured out how stars form new **elements**, with the amount of elements increasing over time. However, unlike other cosmologists of his time, he argued that the universe was constantly expanding but with the same density, an idea he called the "steady state" theory.

A GROWING UNIVERSE

During the first half of the 1900s, astronomers had come to understand that the universe was far larger and older than anyone had previously thought. They had also come to understand far more about how the universe was created.

In 1897, the British physicist Lord Kelvin (1824–1907) proposed that Earth was around 20 million years old. By the 1950s, technological advances allowed geologists, or scientists who study rocks, to prove that it was, in fact, closer to 4.5 billion years old. But that was just the age of Earth itself. How old was the universe Earth was part of?

Fred Hoyle was able to partly answer that question. His studies showed how stars were formed when clouds of gas clumped together under the force of gravity to form a huge **nuclear reaction.** They also showed what happened when the clouds of gas ran out of hydrogen to fuel that reaction. Hoyle showed that these dying stars expanded into red giants, which were many times larger than our Sun. When they had burned all their helium fuel, they collapsed into smaller stars known as white dwarfs. The existence of white dwarfs suggested that the universe has been in existence for billions of years.

This illustration shows planets forming in the disk of dust around a new star.

It was only in 1924, when Edwin Hubble discovered other galaxies, such as Andromeda, that astronomers realized the universe stretched beyond the Milky Way.

Moving galaxies

The question of the age of the universe was central to everything, but it did not answer the question of how it began or whether it was changing. These questions had moved from the world of religion, where the Bible said God had created the universe in six days, to become the concern of physics and math. Physicists were starting to prove that the universe obeyed mathematical laws. In 1917, Albert Einstein proposed that the universe was unchanging, which suggested that it had no origin. But he changed his mind after the American astronomer Edwin Hubble (1889–1953) discovered that what were thought to be clouds of gas in space were actually huge clusters of stars called galaxies.

These galaxies appeared to be moving away from Earth. From that, Hubble concluded in 1929 that everything in the universe is expanding away from everything else. Einstein altered his ideas, but nobody could yet explain the apparent expansion of the universe.

This stamp celebrates the discoveries Edwin Hubble made using Mount Wilson Observatory.

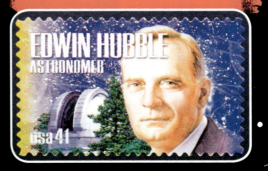

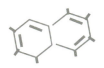

THE BIG BANG

In 1927, a Belgian priest and physicist named Georges Lemaître (1894–1966) came up with the most likely explanation yet of how the universe began. He suggested that a single explosive moment that brought all **matter** and energy into being had created it from nothing. Lemaître had no evidence to back up his theory. That would have to wait until 1964, and the discovery of **radio waves** called cosmic background radiation.

*At some time in the past, all matter had been compressed into a single point, or **singularity**.*

Lemaître thought that the expansion of the universe suggested that, at some time in the past, all matter had been compressed, or squeezed, into a single point. This point is called a singularity, or a point in space-time at the center of a black hole. This singularity expanded, forming the universe. It continues to speed away from the original moment of singularity. Albert Einstein had already suggested that singularities existed. Lemaître called his theory the "**hypothesis** of the **primeval** atom."

This illustration imagines the expansion of the universe from a singularity, shown on the left.

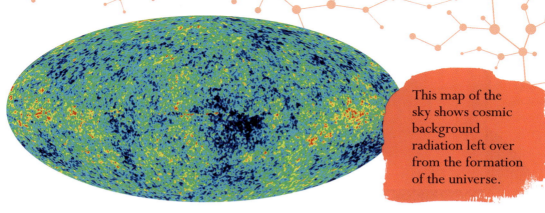

This map of the sky shows cosmic background radiation left over from the formation of the universe.

A cool name

Fred Hoyle gave Lemaître's theory the name by which it is still known: the Big Bang theory. However, Hoyle suggested that, as galaxies moved away from each other, new galaxies were continually formed from new matter to take their place.

Proof of the Big Bang

In 1964, scientists at Cambridge University studied the sources of radio waves known to fill outer space, called cosmic background radiation. They saw that most of the sources of radiation lay outside our galaxy. They then discovered that there were many more weak sources of radio waves than strong sources, and guessed that these weak sources must be much farther from Earth than the strong ones. This suggested that, in the past, all the sources of radio waves had been much closer together. The discovery proved the Big Bang theory and contradicted Hoyle's ideas.

HISTORY'S STORY

In the 1970s, American astronomer Vera Rubin (1928–2016) was studying the Andromeda Galaxy when she noticed that the stars at its edge were spinning so fast they should have been thrown out into space. The galaxy did not have enough **mass** to create enough gravity to hold it together—unless there was invisible matter adding to the galaxy's mass. Rubin called it "dark matter."

ADVANCES IN ASTRONOMY 1900–1970

Stephen Hawking's work came at the end of a period of rapid astronomical advances as follows:

1900 Paul Villard (1860–1934) discovers gamma rays, which are a form of energy that is released as the **nuclei** of atoms decay.

1908 Magnetic fields surrounding sunspots, or dark spots on the Sun's outer shell, are discovered.

1911 Victor Hess (1883–1964) discovers cosmic rays, which are very high-energy particles traveling through space.

1924 Edwin Hubble proves there are other galaxies that lie beyond the Milky Way.

1930 The dwarf planet Pluto is discovered.

1931 Karl Jansky (1905–1950) discovers radio waves coming from the center of the Milky Way galaxy.

1937 Physicists suggest that most of the matter in the universe is "dark matter."

1939 The possible existence of black holes is mentioned.

Pluto was considered a planet until 2006, when it was downgraded to a dwarf planet.

1942 Radio **emissions** from flares on the Sun are discovered.

1957 October 4: The first human-made satellite, the Soviet spacecraft *Sputnik 1*, is launched. The event starts the space race.

1957 November 3: The first animal, Laika the dog, goes into space, onboard the Soviet satellite *Sputnik 2*.

1958 January 31: The first American satellite, *Explorer I*, is launched.

1958 October 1: The National Aeronautical and Space Administration (NASA) is created in the United States.

1959 September 13: The Soviet *Luna II* spacecraft becomes the first human-made device to reach the moon.

1969 July 20: American astronauts on the *Apollo 11* mission walk on the moon.

A statue celebrates Laika, a stray dog fired into space by the Soviet Union.

The *Apollo 11* moon landing was the first of six crewed missions to land on the moon.

CHAPTER 3

In this illustration, a disk of dust and gas swirls around a black hole as it shoots radiation (blue) into space.

STUDYING SPACE
Breakthrough

Hawking's main research interests during his career included:

- The origins of the universe and the Big Bang theory
- Proving the existence of singularities, or the **infinitely** dense points at the center of black holes
- Showing how black holes behave, including the black holes at the center of most galaxies
- Finding a Theory of Everything, to explain the entire universe
- Discovering whether time had a beginning

Hawking said that his discovery that BLACK HOLES emit RADIATION had raised serious PROBLEMS because it did not fit with the rest of PHYSICS. He said he had not SOLVED these problems, but that the ANSWER had turned out not to be what he EXPECTED it to be.

SINGULARITIES

In 1965, Hawking married Jane Wilde, whom he had met not long before he was diagnosed with ALS. Despite his health problems and the birth of a son, Robert, Hawking was still working hard. To get his doctorate degree, he had to research and write a long essay, called a thesis. Hawking decided to work on the origin of the universe. Entitled "Properties of Expanding Universes," his thesis would not defend the "steady state" theory supported by Hoyle. Instead, it would develop the Big Bang theory.

Nobody really knew what a black hole was or what happened inside one.

Hawking wanted to show how the entire mass of the universe might have been contained within a singularity. His inspiration came from another English physicist, Roger Penrose (1931–). Penrose had suggested that the **gravitational pull** at the center of a black hole might be so strong that matter, space, and even time could not escape and was compressed into a singularity. This idea was very new. The name "black hole" had only appeared for the first time in 1963. Nobody really knew what a black hole was or what happened inside one. Hawking realized that, to explain singularities, he needed to combine Einstein's General Theory of Relativity with quantum theory. When he did that, he discovered that black holes could not be completely black, because they would give off radiation before disappearing. This radiation was named Hawking radiation in his honor.

Roger Penrose wondered if a universe existed before the Big Bang that created our current universe.

Ideas that changed the world

Hawking commented that his work with Roger Penrose seemed for years to be a disaster for science, because it appeared to show that science could not explain how the universe began. However, if Einstein's General Theory of Relativity was correct, Hawking said, the universe must have begun with a singularity.

Exploring the ideas

The work Hawking and Penrose did on black holes contradicted all the laws physicists used to explain the structure of the universe. Nobody could predict what would happen at the center of a black hole. In his thesis, Hawking proposed that the **hypothetical** singularity in a hypothetical black hole would be a perfect model for the Big Bang theory. He suggested that all the matter that had ever existed in the universe had once been compressed into a single point. When this singularity exploded, matter was released and created the universe. Today, this idea is widely accepted, but in the 1960s it was very **radical**.

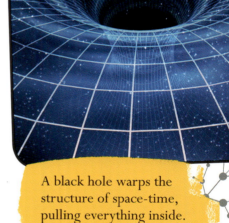

A black hole warps the structure of space-time, pulling everything inside.

HISTORY'S STORY

Hawking's discovery of black hole radiation in 1974 earned him an invitation to become a fellow of the Royal Society. The Royal Society, founded in 1660 in London, England, is the world's oldest scientific academy. All the leading British scientists of the past have belonged to the Royal Society, including Sir Isaac Newton, who served as president.

RAPID EXPANSION

By 1979, Stephen Hawking's work was respected around the world. His fellow professors at Cambridge had voted him Lucasian Professor of Mathematics. The position is the highest honor a teacher of math and science can be given. Sir Isaac Newton had once held the same position. By then, Hawking's health had worsened. He had been using a wheelchair for 10 years, but that did not stop him from working. The next question he wanted to answer was what happened in the moments after the Big Bang.

During the 1970s, physicists were starting to come up with theories to answer that question. In 1979, American scientist Alan Guth suggested that right after the Big Bang the universe went through a period of incredibly fast expansion he called **"inflationary."** Guth's theory was that in only a fraction of a fraction of a second, the size of the universe increased by a million trillion trillion times. The rapid expansion was called **cosmological inflation**. The universe then settled down to a slower rate of expansion.

Hawking was very excited by Guth's ideas. In the summer of 1982, he organized a three-week workshop in Cambridge where leading physicists came together to focus on this theory. Hawking began a new line of research into the universe's origins.

Hawking tried to simplify his theories by using comparisons such as bubbles on the surface of water.

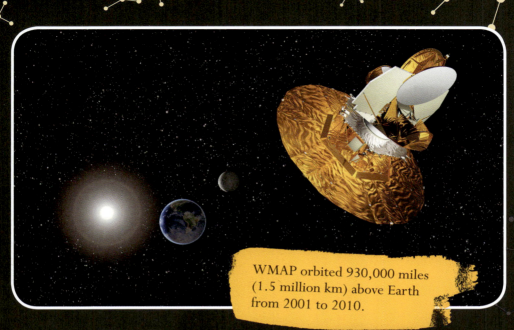

WMAP orbited 930,000 miles (1.5 million km) above Earth from 2001 to 2010.

The very early universe

Hawking's work on inflation suggested that the universe did not expand in a symmetrical, or consistently balanced way. Instead, it was full of irregularities. Hawking described the universe's origins in terms of bubbles on the surface of water, which appear and burst. In the same way, he suggested, many **microscopic** universes might have appeared. They then burst, like bubbles, before they could grow. Working together with four other groups of physicists, Hawking used quantum physics to prove that the universe had started this way—in a microscopic form that rapidly grew.

The proof

In 2006, a NASA spacecraft named the Wilkinson Microwave Anisotropy Probe (WMAP) measured temperature differences across space, and the heat left behind after the Big Bang. The temperature differences suggested that Hawking's theory was true. This also proved that Hawking had been correct in his attempt to combine Einstein's General Theory of Relativity with quantum physics. The Theory of Relativity predicted that singularities existed. It gave Hawking the model to figure out how singularities—and the Big Bang itself—came about.

AN ENDLESS UNIVERSE

In 1981, after working on the moment after the Big Bang, Hawking came up with a bold new idea. He suggested that the universe had no boundaries: there was no beginning, no end, and no edges. He also suggested that time would reverse if the universe started contracting, or getting smaller. However, when his suggestion was shown to be wrong, he withdrew the idea.

Since Galileo Galilei in the 1600s, the method used by scientists is to test every idea again and again with experiments. Modern scientists take for granted that any new theory has to be tested many times. However, Hawking believed that this was not possible in the area of physics and cosmology in which he worked. Concrete proof that an idea was correct was not always available. Instead, Hawking liked to **speculate**, then to use math to try to show how his idea might work. Many of his ideas were so far ahead of technology that there was no way to prove them.

Even though he was considered to be one of the leading physicists of his time, Hawking did not always get things right. When he got things wrong, he knew the most important thing was to admit the mistake, then to go back and reassess the data to see if he could learn anything from it.

The Hubble Space Telescope revealed hundreds of galaxies at the far reaches of the known universe.

Time reversing

Having explored the start of the universe, Hawking also wondered what would happen to it at the end of time. In a paper in 1985, he suggested that, if the no-boundary theory was correct, then once the universe stopped expanding, it would eventually collapse and time would run backward.

The idea was based on several assumptions. Hawking and his colleague James Hartle argued that, if we traveled back to when the universe began, there would be only space and no time near the beginning. If time does not exist, there could be no beginning. As time did not exist before the Big Bang, they argued, the concept of time is meaningless and there are no boundaries in the universe in either space or time. That point led Hawking to conclude that, once the universe stopped expanding, time would reverse.

If time could run backward, would it mean that it was possible to travel into the past?

However, when Raymond Laflamme, one of Hawking's PhD students, did the math, he persuaded Hawking that he was wrong. Time would not reverse in a contracting universe. Hawking was convinced by his student, and withdrew his idea.

HAWKING'S FELLOW SCIENTISTS

Stephen Hawking lived at the same time as many outstanding physicists. He worked with some of them over his career, and acknowledged the other scientists whose ideas had influenced his own.

James B. Hartle (1939–)

The American physicist and professor worked with Hawking to explain the conditions necessary for the Big Bang. He is known for his work on general relativity, **astrophysics**, and interpreting quantum physics.

Richard P. Feynman (1918–1988)

Widely seen as a genius and the most **influential** American physicist of his generation, Feynman won the Nobel Prize for Physics in 1965. He was best known for his work in quantum physics. His "Feynman diagrams" were drawings of math equations that described the behavior of subatomic particles. He worked on developing the **atomic bomb** during **World War II**.

Richard Feynman wrote books to explain physics to non-scientists.

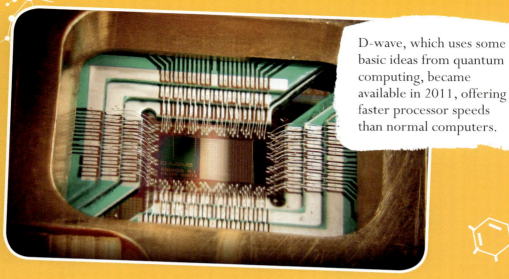

D-wave, which uses some basic ideas from quantum computing, became available in 2011, offering faster processor speeds than normal computers.

Sir Roger Penrose (1931–)

An English mathematical physicist who works on general relativity and cosmology, Penrose **revolutionized** the mathematical tools that we use to analyze the properties of space-time. He worked with Stephen Hawking and has calculated many of the basic features of black holes.

Raymond Laflamme (1960–)

A Canadian physicist whose PhD was supervised by Hawking, Laflamme is famous for his work on quantum computing. This is a form of computer that is based on the behavior of atoms. In 2005, his research team created the world's largest quantum information processor.

Alan Guth (1947–)

The American theoretical physicist and cosmologist developed the idea of cosmic inflation in 1979. He won a major scientific honor called the Kavli Prize for it in 2014. He has researched how particle theory, which covers the tiny particles that make up matter, can be applied to the very early universe.

CHAPTER 4

This bench in London celebrated Hawking's book *A Brief History of Time*.

A BRIEF HISTORY OF TIME
Spreading Ideas

Stephen Hawking's bestselling book, *A Brief History of Time*, was published in 1988. Here are some of the key ideas:

Big Bang theory: How the universe began

Space-time: Hawking's theories on the relationship between space and time

Gravity: Building on the work of Isaac Newton and Albert Einstein

Elementary particles: The nature of the tiniest and most basic building blocks that make up the universe. They are particles that cannot be divided.

Expanding universe: How the universe is increasing in size

Black holes: What they are and what they mean

Fate of the universe: Ideas about what will happen to the universe

Hawking said that HUMANITY'S deep desire to gain KNOWLEDGE was enough to justify the STUDIES of SCIENTISTS. Humanity's GOAL was nothing less than being able to completely EXPLAIN the WHOLE UNIVERSE.

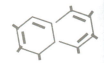

A BESTSELLING BOOK

In 1982, Hawking decided to write a science book that explained the universe not just to other physicists, but to anyone who was interested. He wanted it to be the kind of book people might buy at an airport bookstore. That book was *A Brief History of Time*.

In 1984, Hawking sent a draft of his book to various publishers. He was very eager for one publisher in particular to take it. Bantam Press printed the kind of popular books that Hawking wanted his book to be. Bantam said it would publish the book, but when the editor read the draft, he told Hawking he had to rewrite it so that non-scientists could understand it. That meant leaving out the complicated math equations.

This stamp showing Hawking was released in the Isle of Man in 2016.

By then, however, Hawking's disease had advanced so much that he could no longer use his hands. To write, he had to use a computer that he controlled by moving the small muscles near his eyes. Writing that way was very slow. He could write only 15 words a minute, but he was so determined that he rewrote the whole text. His editor sent it off to other scientists to check for errors. Once they had been corrected, the book was ready for publication. It appeared on the shelves in 1988. Since then, the book has sold more than 10 million copies.

Ideas that changed the world

Hawking believed that science did not need to be scary or hard. He believed science was beautiful when it provided simple explanations or drew the link between two seemingly unconnected things. For him, physics equations were beautiful.

Exploring the ideas

Before *A Brief History of Time* was published, the study of the universe was something that was discussed only by scientists. They were usually scientists who specialized in one area. The ideas behind the origin of the universe, space, and time were so complicated that most people thought only physicists, astrophysicists, and cosmologists had any clue how to think about them. Hawking's great genius was to open the debate up to everyone and also to show us just how extraordinary, fascinating, and enchanting science—and the universe—really are.

Hawking's speech **synthesize**r (pictured) sounded robotic and had an American accent. Hawking did not care: at least he had a voice again.

HISTORY'S STORY

While writing *A Brief History of Time*, Hawking almost died of **pneumonia**. After surgery to save his life, he lost the ability to speak. Walter Woltosz was a Californian computer expert whose mother-in-law had suffered the same loss of voice. Woltosz created a computer program for Hawking that allowed him to choose words with a switch controlled by his thumb.

THE FACE OF SCIENCE

The success of *A Brief History of Time* made Stephen Hawking one of the best-known scientists in the world. His wheelchair and robotic voice meant that he was instantly recognized wherever he went and whenever he spoke. Overnight, he had become a media star in demand across the globe.

Hawking had always traveled to attend conferences and explain his research. This time was different. Now people wanted to meet him because he was the author of a bestselling book who was also severely disabled. There was nobody like Stephen Hawking. Always one to enjoy a party and meet new people, Hawking was eager to accept as many invitations as his health permitted.

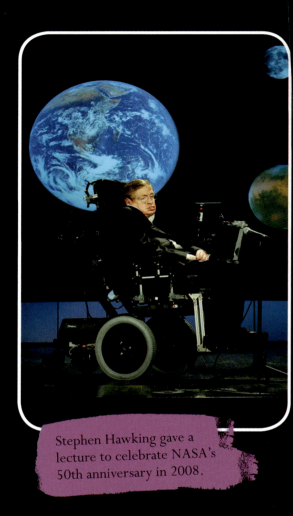

Stephen Hawking gave a lecture to celebrate NASA's 50th anniversary in 2008.

Meantime, Hawking's personal life was changing. Jane and he now had three children together: Robert, Lucy, and Timothy. As Hawking's ALS advanced, not only was Jane working and looking after the children, but she also took on the demanding task of caregiving for her husband. After he almost died from pneumonia, it was clear Hawking needed round-the-clock care. A team of nurses came to their house to help.

Separation

Jane had already been feeling isolated, and now Hawking's constant traveling did not help. It had been clear for a long time that the couple were drifting apart and, in 1990, they separated. Hawking moved in with his nurse, Elaine, who had been with him as he flew around Europe and the United States to promote *A Brief History of Time*. In 1995, Jane and Stephen divorced and he married Elaine.

Back to work

The constant traveling and meeting people meant that there was little time to spare for Hawking to concentrate on his work. Meanwhile, other physicists and cosmologists were continuing to work on their own theories that advanced our knowledge about the universe. Mathematical evidence proved that the universe was not only getting bigger but that the edges of the universe were moving away from each other. It was time to get back to work. Hawking turned his attention to black holes and the theory that the universe was expanding. The math for black holes worked with the math for an expanding universe.

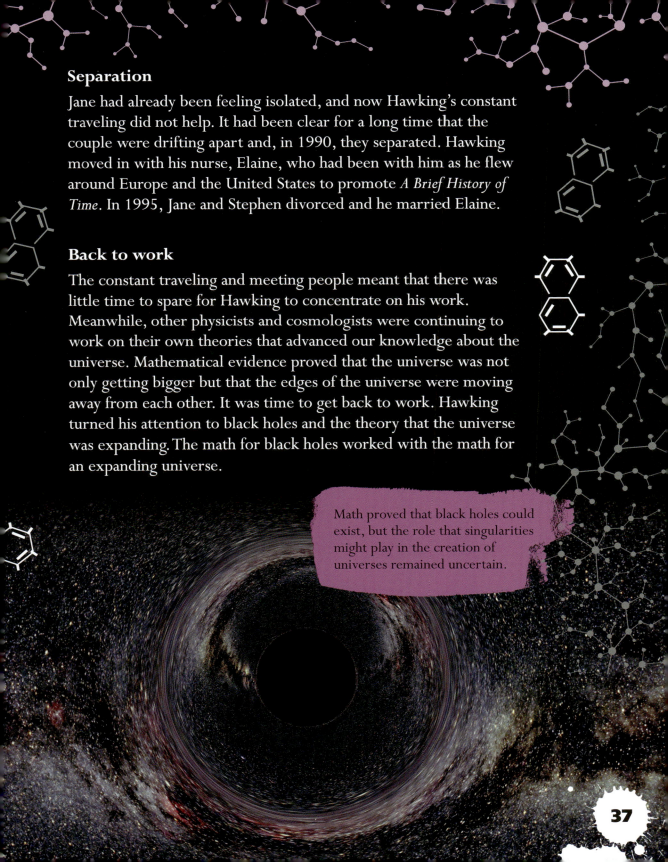

Math proved that black holes could exist, but the role that singularities might play in the creation of universes remained uncertain.

PLACING BETS

Hawking worked during a very exciting time for physicists and cosmologists. New theories were brought forward all the time. Sometimes, new ideas contradicted each other and scientists disagreed. When that happened, Hawking liked to bet with his fellow scientists on the outcome of different theories.

One of the longest disagreements Hawking had with a fellow scientist was whether the Higgs boson would ever be found. The Higgs boson is an elementary particle, or a particle that is not made of any other particles. Its existence was first suggested by the British theoretical physicist Peter Higgs (1929–) in 1964. Higgs said that there must be an elementary particle that gave everything in the universe mass. Hawking disagreed and the two men had heated debates over many years about whether the "boson" would ever be found. Hawking bet that it would not. He was proven wrong.

The Large Hadron Collider uses magnets to accelerate atoms around a 16.8-mile (27-km) ring.

In July 2012, the particle was discovered at the **European Organization for Nuclear Research (CERN)** in Switzerland. The discovery followed the building of the **particle accelerator** called the Large Hadron Collider. Particle accelerators drive particles at very high speeds. Hawking was quick to admit he had lost his bet and said he thought Higgs should be awarded the Nobel Prize for Physics. Higgs did win the prize the following year.

Without a trace

Hawking proved that black holes existed, but important questions about them still remained. Decades earlier, Hawking's calculations had shown that radiation escapes the event horizon of a black hole. The event horizon is the boundary of a black hole, inside of which not even light can escape. He thought this radiation should eventually destroy any trace that the black hole ever existed. Scientists disagreed about whether this could happen, because it should be forbidden by the laws of quantum physics.

Over the decades, scientists such as John Preskill argued that Hawking must be wrong. A long-running bet started in 1997 between Preskill and Hawking and his colleague Kip Thorne. In 2004, Hawking announced he had lost the bet because he thought that black holes must leave evidence of their existence. Preskill refused to accept Hawking's defeat because he said the case had not been proven. Hawking continued to work on the proof.

Subatomic particles such as the Higgs boson can be seen in the patterns formed when atoms collide in a particle accelerator.

HISTORY'S STORY

The success of *A Brief History of Time* convinced Hawking that there was an appetite for scientific knowledge among the general public. His daughter Lucy and he decided to write a series of children's science books. The hero and heroine, George and Annie, have adventures in space, teaching kids about theoretical physics in a fun way.

HAWKING'S KEY WRITINGS

"Singularities and the Geometry of Space-Time" (1966)
Hawking's essay won the Adams Prize.

The Large Scale Structure of Space-Time (1973)
This was a textbook for physicists rather than for general readers.

A Brief History of Time (1988)
This groundbreaking bestseller set out to explain physics and the universe to non-scientists, without using math equations.

Black Holes and Baby Universes and Other Essays (1993)
This included 13 essays that looked at the latest understanding of the universe.

The Universe in a Nutshell (2001)
Using illustrations, the book explained many of the concepts in *A Brief History of Time* that readers had found difficult to understand.

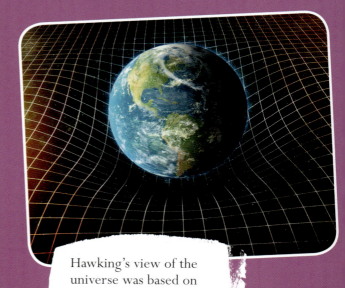

Hawking's view of the universe was based on Einstein's idea that time and space were like a sheet that could be bent by the gravity of large objects.

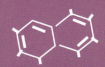

A Briefer History of Time (2005)
This set out to explain the key ideas in the much longer 1988 book.

God Created the Integers (2005)
Hawking presented the work of mathematicians from Euclid to Alan Turing, whose breakthroughs had changed history.

George's Secret Key to the Universe (2007)
Written with Hawking's daughter Lucy, this was the first of a series of children's science fiction books about the universe.

The Grand Design (2010)
In this book, Hawking discussed a theory known as the M-Theory, which predicts that there are many universes and that there is no Theory of Everything to describe our particular universe.

My Brief History (2013)
This was Hawking's autobiography, from his childhood to his days as a world-famous scientist.

"A Smooth Exit from Eternal Inflation?" (2017)
Hawking's last published scientific paper tackled the idea of a multiverse, or many universes existing at the same time.

According to the M-Theory, there are many parallel universes—and possibly an infinite number.

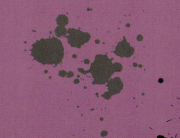

41

CHAPTER 5
INTERNATIONAL PROFILE
Reputation

Hawking and his daughter, Lucy, meet with President Barack Obama.

Hawking was widely acknowledged as an outstanding scientist and received many awards and honors:

1979: Becomes Lucasian Professor of Mathematics at Cambridge University. He is only the 17th person to hold the position, which he keeps for the next 30 years.

1982: Queen Elizabeth II awards him a CBE (Commander of the Order of the British Empire).

1989: He is made a member of the Order of the Companions of Honour. There are only 66 members allowed at any time, including the Sovereign, or ruler, of the United Kingdom.

2009: President Barack Obama awards him the Presidential Medal of Freedom, the highest civilian honor in the United States.

2012: He is awarded the Fundamental Physics Prize of $3 million for his theory on the ability of black holes to emit energy.

Hawking said that no SCIENTIST started research in PHYSICS in order to win a PRIZE but to experience the JOY of DISCOVERING something that NO ONE has ever known before.

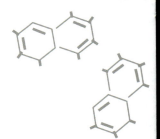

OVERCOMING DISABILITY

As one of the most recognized people in the world, Hawking took on an **unintentional** but important role as a figurehead. He showed that it was possible to overcome severe disability, and that physical disability was no indication of a person's intelligence.

Given only two years to live… Hawking went on to defy medical experts' expectations.

Despite Hawking being frequently sick when he was a child, there was nothing in the Hawking family's medical history to suggest that he would get incurable ALS just before his 21st birthday. Given only two years to live when he was originally diagnosed, Hawking went on to defy medical experts' expectations. He showed that it was possible to live an extremely full life despite having what was called a life-limiting disease.

Hawking's fame boosted the confidence of many young people with disabilities.

Hawking was always at the cutting edge of science. After 1969, once he lost the use of his legs and it became too hard to use crutches, he went everywhere in a wheelchair. The chair was regularly updated so he had the latest model to make his life as comfortable as possible. In the same way, after 1985, Hawking communicated using a groundbreaking speech program.

Ideas that changed the world

Hawking said that his advice to other people with disabilities was to concentrate on things their disability did not prevent them from doing well, and not to regret the things it interfered with. They should not be disabled in spirit as well as physically.

Exploring the ideas

Hawking lived his own advice. His disability was a constant frustration, but he tried not to let it get in his way. As he grew older, he noticed that life for disabled people in Britain got easier compared to when he was younger. Laws that attempted to ensure more equality between disabled people and non-disabled people helped. Disabled access ramps became standard in many buildings across Britain. Even though it was easier to get around, however, there was no escape for Hawking from the limitations his body placed on his daily life. He needed constant nursing help and he knew that any illness might kill him.

After his weightless flight, Hawking said, "Space, here I come."

HISTORY'S STORY

Hawking dreamed of going into space so he could be weightless to escape the pressures on his body. In 2007, he became the first quadriplegic, or person who cannot use their arms and legs, to take a zero-gravity flight on a special airliner that re-creates weightlessness. It was not quite space, but it was the next best thing.

SCIENCE FICTION?

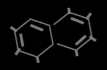

Many of Hawking's ideas were hard for most people to grasp, but some were far easier. When he was not thinking about theoretical and quantum physics, Hawking liked to think about more popular questions, such as whether alien life exists. He wondered if time travel is possible, and whether humans could ever move to live on other planets.

Hawking grew more concerned about the threat we face from meeting alien civilizations. He argued that aliens were probably advanced enough to travel to Earth and that there was a good chance they would be hostile. He thought efforts to try to contact aliens were a bad idea because they might colonize Earth, just as Europeans had colonized other parts of our planet in the past. He pointed to what happened to Indigenous peoples when European settlers arrived on their continents.

Hawking warned scientists that sending signals into the universe might attract aliens who would destroy life on Earth.

Some of Hawking's fellow scientists thought he was being silly. They argued that we have been sending out signals to outer space for a long time now, so any aliens out there would know where to come. The fact they had not appeared suggested that, if they did exist, they could not travel through space.

Time travel

Hawking believed that travel into the future was a possibility. He argued that it happens all the time. Einstein's General Theory of Relativity says that, the closer an object approaches the speed of light, the more it moves into the future relative to its starting point. A rocket that traveled close to the speed of light could theoretically project a person forward in time. However, the faster it went, the more mass the rocket would take on. To go almost as fast as the speed of light, the rocket's mass would have to increase so much it would barely fit into the universe!

Moving to exoplanets

Overpopulation, the threat of nuclear weapons, and the damage to our planet due to global warming made Hawking very worried about humanity's future. He thought that the best hope humankind had was to try to colonize the closest exoplanets, which are planets outside our solar system. The only way to do that was by sending spacecraft to see if anywhere else in space had conditions that would support life. In 2016, Hawking told an audience at the launch of the Breakthrough Starshot project, which plans to travel to other solar systems, that time was running out for humanity, which needed to look for a new home.

> Hawking's belief that humans might move to other planets is, so far, only possible in science fiction.

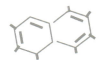

LAST YEARS

Stephen Hawking worked right up until his death on March 14, 2018. Just 10 days earlier, he published an update of his last paper. When Hawking's death was announced, the world was shocked as it had seemed as though he would carry on defying his body forever. For a man who had been told he had two years to live when he was 20, he had enjoyed a long life. There was an outpouring of sadness at the passing of one of the most remarkable scientists and men to have ever lived.

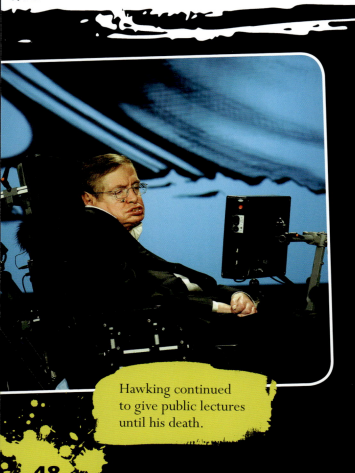

Hawking continued to give public lectures until his death.

In 2009, in line with the rules at Cambridge University, Hawking stepped down from his position as Lucasian Professor of Mathematics after holding the position for 30 years. But that did not mean he was retiring. Hawking returned to doing what he most enjoyed: thinking about the universe.

In 2012, Hawking was awarded the Fundamental Physics Prize, which came with $3 million. It was a large amount, but with a number of bestselling books already behind him, it had been a long time since Hawking had to worry about money. He had published another bestseller, *The Grand Design*, in 2010.

Traveling the world

Hawking and his second wife, Elaine, divorced in 2006. He never remarried. He remained close friends with his first wife, Jane, and spent a lot of time with his three children and his grandchildren. He spent much of his last 10 years traveling the world, attending scientific conferences and meeting all kinds of people, including President Barack Obama and Nelson Mandela, who was president of South Africa between 1994 and 1999.

Some experts warn that artificial intelligence might take over from human intelligence.

Speaking for the future

Hawking also used his position as the world's most famous scientist to comment on all kinds of issues about which he felt passionately, including global warming and the threat that artificial intelligence (AI) might pose. AI is programming that allows computers to carry out tasks normally done by humans. Like some other leading scientists, Hawking believed that AI could spell the end of the human race because AI has the technology to develop and change at a much faster rate than humans can evolve.

HISTORY'S STORY

In April 2012, Stephen Hawking appeared on the comedy show *The Big Bang Theory*. The show tells the stories of two brilliant physicists, Leonard and Sheldon, who know how the universe works but little about how to function in daily life. For many younger viewers, this was the first time they had heard of Hawking. More than 13 million people tuned in to watch.

HAWKING ON SCREEN

Appearing as Himself

***Star Trek: The Next Generation* (1993)** He played himself as a hologram in the last episode of Season 6.

***The Simpsons* (1999–2010)** Providing his own voice, he appeared in cartoon form in four episodes.

***Futurama* (2000)** He appeared in Season 2 of the cartoon show created by Matt Groening, who also created *The Simpsons*.

***The Big Bang Theory* (2012–2017)** He appeared in a number of episodes of the long-running comedy.

In one of Hawking's appearances on *The Simpsons*, Homer tells him the universe is donut shaped.

Shows and Movies about Hawking

***A Brief History of Time* (1991)** This was the first biography of Hawking, with contributions from him, his friends, family, and colleagues.

***Hawking* (2004)** This BBC movie was about Hawking's life in Cambridge. He was played by Benedict Cumberbatch.

***Hawking* (2013)** A documentary about Hawking's life, this movie was narrated by him and those closest to him.

***The Theory of Everything* (2014)** This movie focused on Hawking's time with his first wife, Jane. Stephen was played by Eddie Redmayne, who won an Oscar for his performance.

Documentaries by Hawking

***Stephen Hawking's Universe* (1997)** In this documentary, he looked at the entire universe from the Big Bang to the end of time.

***Into the Universe with Stephen Hawking* (2010)** Billed as a *Planet Earth* for the universe, this was Hawking's guide to the universe.

***Stephen Hawking's Grand Design* (2012)** Hawking addressed many of the key questions of physics and cosmology, drawing on 40 years of research and breakthroughs.

Eddie Redmayne played Hawking on film and later gave a reading at his funeral.

CHAPTER 6

Scientists know that a mysterious dark energy helps shape the universe—but they do not what it is or how it works.

PUSHING KNOWLEDGE
Legacy

Some of the areas of ongoing physics research include:

- Continuing Hawking's research to establish that dark matter is not made up of tiny black holes
- Investigating why the universe's expansion is accelerating
- Studying dark matter, which makes up 85 percent of the matter in the universe
- Studying dark energy, which makes up approximately 68 percent of the energy in universe and acts in opposition to gravity
- Devising a successful theory of quantum gravity, which tries to describe gravity in terms of the behavior of atoms and subatomic particles

Hawking said that HUMANKIND should commit to searching for LIFE BEYOND EARTH. He believed humans have a deep need to EXPLORE, to LEARN, and to KNOW. It is important for us to know if we are ALONE in the DARK.

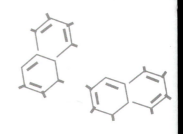

PHYSICS ON THE AGENDA

During his life, Stephen Hawking did what seemed impossible. He took a "geeky" subject—theoretical physics—out of universities and into people's homes. *A Brief History of Time* was a huge hit, and shows such as *The Simpsons* and *The Big Bang Theory*, watched by millions, had Hawking as a guest. Who would have thought that a physics professor would become a media star?

Hawking liked to speculate creatively about the big questions.

In the century since Einstein delivered his Theory of Relativity, the world of physics has expanded massively. The realization that there is a whole new dimension of the universe that is described by quantum physics has shown physicists that there is still a lot to learn. At the same time, there have been advances in computing and equipment such as telescopes and particle accelerators. Hawking liked to speculate creatively about the big questions. This was an **unorthodox** approach, but his discoveries proved that it worked. The same creative approach means that physicists today are in great demand from the financial and computing industries.

This illustration shows the patterns made by particles in a particle accelerator.

Ideas that changed the world

Hawking said that he hoped he had been able to raise the profile of science and to show everyone that physics is not a mystery but something that could be understood by everyone.

Exploring the ideas

Few people would disagree that Stephen Hawking played a unique role in bringing physics to the general public. From his bestselling books that explained complex physics in as simple terms as possible to his TV appearances and the movies made about his life, Hawking combined a popular approach with serious scientific studies. Thanks to him, everybody has heard of black holes and knows—a little—about how they behave.

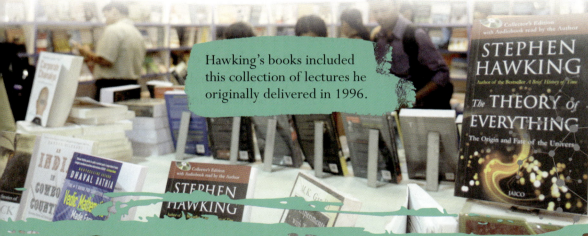

Hawking's books included this collection of lectures he originally delivered in 1996.

HISTORY'S STORY

In 1954, an international laboratory was established by CERN in Switzerland. CERN built the Large Hadron Collider particle accelerator. Opened in 2008, it takes the form of an underground ring with a circumference of 16.8 miles (27 km). It smashes atoms into one another at high speeds to learn about the elemental particles that may explain the origins of the universe.

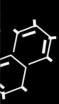

SPACE EXPLORATION

The future of space exploration looks exciting. Astronomers are trying a number of different approaches. These include telescopic exploration, uncrewed robotic space **probes**, and a return to human spaceflights. In the past, it was the United States and the Soviet Union that led the way. Today, China, India, and Europe are all key players in space exploration.

Telescopic exploration

Since the days of Galileo, telescopes have advanced to the point that they can see clear visual or radio images of objects trillions of miles away. NASA's latest telescope, the James Webb Space Telescope, was planned to be launched in 2021. It will take over from the aging Hubble Space Telescope and travel a million miles from Earth to orbit the Sun and send back images. In the meantime, Hubble continues to send back remarkable images from outer space, including images of galaxies 55,000 light-years away. A light-year is the distance light can travel in one year.

The collection of mirrors that capture light on the James Webb Space Telescope will be more than 21 feet (6.4 m) wide.

Space probes

Ever since the Soviet Union launched the first satellite in 1957, different nations have sent probes into space. Our nearest planets, such as Jupiter and Venus, are not suitable for human life. Robotic space probes are the best way to visit them and collect data. Planets such as Saturn, Neptune, and Uranus are just too far away for humans to reach, so uncrewed space probes are the only way to explore them. In January 2019, China landed an uncrewed space probe on the far side of the Moon. This was the first time any nation had successfully landed on that side of the Moon.

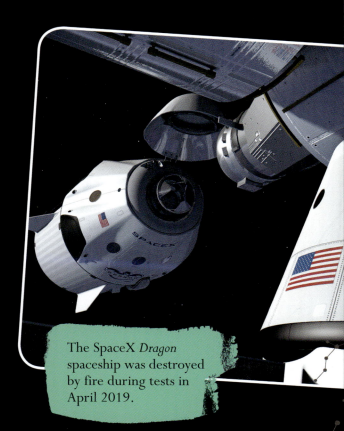

The SpaceX *Dragon* spaceship was destroyed by fire during tests in April 2019.

Crewed missions

The biggest change since the United States and the Soviet Union competed to put the first human on the Moon in the 1960s is that private companies are now launching crewed space missions alongside governments. China, Russia, India, and the United States are among the nations that have crewed space programs planned. Private companies such as SpaceX and Virgin Galactic have programs to send ordinary people into space. So far, eight people have traveled into space with private companies. The cost? Between $20 and $40 million a launch!

The International Space Station

Since 2000, astronauts from 18 different nations and a few space tourists have lived for up to six months on the International Space Station. The station is in orbit around Earth where it experiences 11.25 days for every Earth day. The station is used to carry out research in medicine, weather, and physics.

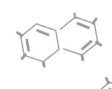

THE NATURE OF MATTER

One of the most exciting areas of research for physicists today was an area that Stephen Hawking was passionate about. What is the universe made of? Ever since the ancient Greeks, more than 2,000 years ago, humans have speculated about the building blocks that make up our universe.

Ever since the **chemist** Robert Boyle (1627–1691) first suggested that gases were made up of tiny particles, scientists have tried to figure out just what those tiny particles might be. When the Danish physicist Niels Bohr (1885–1962) developed a model of an atom, he won the Nobel Prize for Physics in 1922. Bohr imagined an atom in which a nucleus of **protons** and **neutrons** was orbited by a number of **electrons**. The idea launched a whole new branch of physics, called quantum physics.

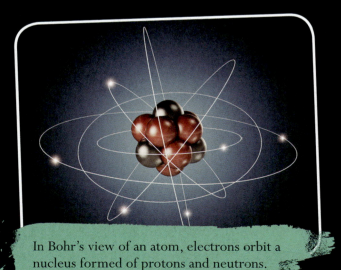

In Bohr's view of an atom, electrons orbit a nucleus formed of protons and neutrons.

Niels Bohr suggested that subatomic particles could behave as particles and waves at the same time.

Dark matter

Scientists now know that the universe contains not only matter, which we can see and measure, but also dark matter, which we cannot. Galaxies move at such a speed that, according to the laws of physics, the gravity generated by the matter we can see could not hold them together. Scientists say there must be something else holding the galaxies together: dark matter, which is not visible. The only way we know dark matter exists is from the gravitational effect it has on visible matter. Dark matter is important, because scientists say it makes up around 85 percent of the matter in the universe. In contrast, the matter that makes up the stars and planets accounts for just 5 percent. The next big challenge for physicists is to find out what dark matter is. They hope that experiments at CERN's Large Hadron Collider might tell them.

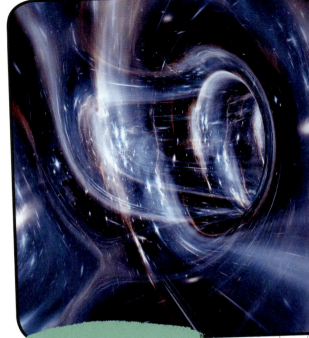

The shape of the universe suggests it contains far more matter than we can see, so scientists believe the missing mass is made up of "dark matter," imagined here by an illustrator.

HISTORY'S STORY

While dark matter produces gravity, a mysterious force called dark energy produces a theoretical force called antigravity, which opposes the force of gravity. Dark energy makes up 68 percent of the energy in the universe. Despite this, little is known about dark energy. Physicists think it is the force that is making the universe expand faster and faster.

UNANSWERED QUESTIONS

Stephen Hawking advanced our understanding of the universe more than any other scientist of his day. After his death, however, some important physics mysteries still remain to be solved.

Size of the universe: We still do not know just how big the universe is. Is it still expanding and, if so, by how much?

Exact age of the universe: Until the mid-20th century, it was thought the universe was 20 million years old. We now know the Sun is at least 4.5 billion years old, but not the exact age of the rest of the universe. Scientists' best guesses are that it is more than 13 billion years old.

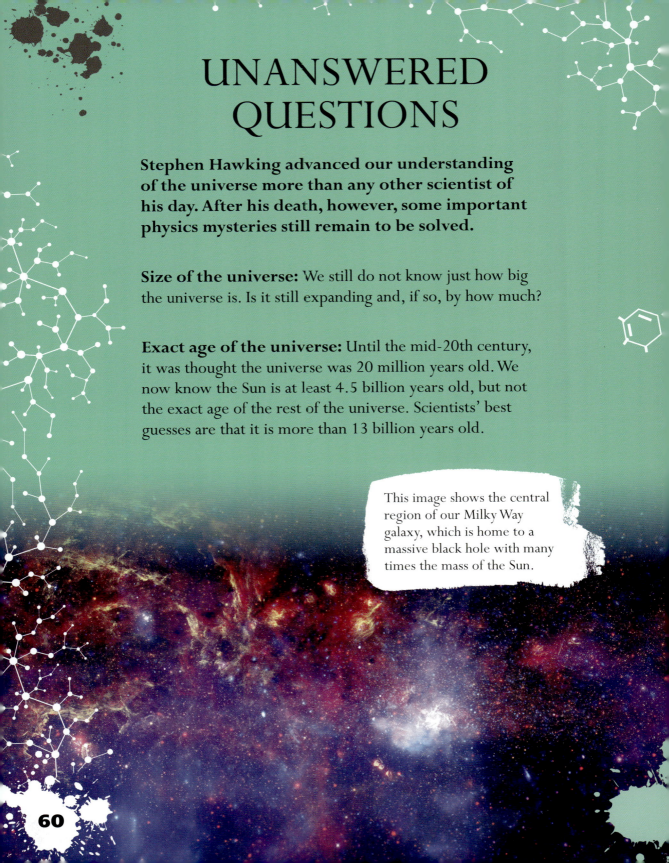

This image shows the central region of our Milky Way galaxy, which is home to a massive black hole with many times the mass of the Sun.

This image taken by the Hubble Space Telescope shows a ghostly ring of dark matter surrounding a distant cluster of galaxies.

The behavior of black holes: There is still a lot to discover about black holes. How can we predict how long a black hole will exist before it explodes? What function did black holes have, if any, in the creation of galaxies? What happens at the event horizon of a black hole?

Proof of dark energy: Physicists are pretty sure that dark energy exists, but they want to find proof. Impossible to see, it is associated with vacuum (seemingly completely empty) space and can only be detected by its effects, such as bending light through the gravity of invisible objects.

Composition of dark matter: Scientists think that dark matter is everywhere in the universe and had a large influence on its structure and development. They think it is made up of some as yet unknown elementary particle. But what?

GLOSSARY

ancestors People from whom others are descended
astronomer A scientist who studies the stars, planets, and space
astrophysics A branch of science that studies the behavior and properties of stars and space
atomic bomb A powerful bomb that uses nuclear energy
atoms The smallest parts of an element that can exist independently
Big Bang The theory that the universe was created from a tiny pinprick in a vast explosion
black holes Regions of space from which nothing can escape, not even light, space, and time, because their gravity is so strong
chemist A scientist who studies substances
cosmological inflation A theory of the rapid expansion of the universe just after the Big Bang
electrons Negatively charged subatomic particles that orbit the nucleus of an atom
elements The 118 substances, such as hydrogen and oxygen, that cannot be broken down into other substances
emissions Things that are released, or given off
European Organization for Nuclear Research (CERN) An international center for physics research
galaxy A system of millions or billions of stars, gas, and dust held together by gravity
gravitational pull The attraction an object exerts on other objects
gravity A force that pulls all objects toward one another
hypothesis An idea based on scientific observation
hypothetical Based on a hypothesis, or idea, but not necessarily true
infinitely Without limit
inflationary Growing bigger quickly
influential Having a strong effect on others
mass Weight
matter Physical substance
medieval During the Middle Ages
microscopic Visible only with a microscope
Middle Ages A period of time from 1100 C.E. to about 1450 C.E.
motor neuron disease A group of disorders that affect the cells that control the muscles of the body
neutrons Subatomic particles that are in the nucleus of most atoms and have no electric charge
nuclear reaction A process in which the nuclei of two atoms collide, producing a different product from the initial particles
nuclei (singular: nucleus) The central part of an atom, made up of protons and neutrons
particle accelerator A machine for sending subatomic particles at very high speeds so that they collide with each other
particles Tiny pieces of matter
physics The branch of science concerned with the nature and properties of matter and energy
pneumonia A serious lung infection
potential Having the ability to develop
primeval The earliest
probes Uncrewed spacecraft
protons Positively charged subatomic particles that are in the nucleus of most atoms
quantum physics Also known as quantum mechanics, the branch of science that focuses on the tiny particles inside atoms
quantum theory A theory of matter and energy based on quantum physics
radical Something that departs from tradition or established ideas
radio waves Waves of energy
revolutionized To radically or fundamentally change something
singularity A point in space-time where matter is infinitely dense, as at the center of a black hole
speculate To form a theory without firm evidence
subatomic particles Particles that are smaller than atoms
synthesizer A machine that produces sound electronically
theory Ideas intended to explain something
Theory of Relativity, General Albert Einstein's theory that explains how gravity can bend four-dimensional space-time
unintentional Not having been meant
unorthodox Not what is usual or accepted
World War II (1939–1945) A war in which the Axis Powers of Germany, Italy, and Japan were defeated by an alliance that included the United Kingdom, the United States, Canada, and the Soviet Union

FOR MORE INFORMATION

BOOKS

Hawking, Stephen, and Lucy Hawking. *George's Secret Key Paperback Collection*. New York, NY: Simon and Schuster Books for Young Readers, 2016.

Roland, James. *Black Holes: A Space Discovery Guide* (Space Discovery Guides). Minneapolis, MN: Lerner Publications, 2017.

Snedden, Robert. *Stephen Hawking: Master of the Cosmos* (Superheroes of Science). New York, NY: Gareth Stevens, 2015.

Wood, Alix. *Stephen Hawking* (World-Changing Scientists). New York, NY: PowerKids Press, 2019.

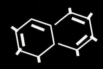

WEBSITES

Black Holes—https://bit.ly/2UzGBbt
A page that explains the mysterious nature of black holes.

Dark Matter—https://spaceplace.nasa.gov/dark-matter/en
An explanation of how scientists know that dark matter exists.

Fun Facts—https://bit.ly/3asZ00c
A collection of interesting facts about Stephen Hawking.

Timeline—www.bbc.com/timelines/zwjmtfr
A timeline of Stephen Hawking's life and work.

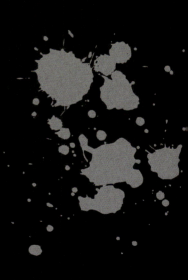

Publisher's note to educators and parents: Our editors have carefully reviewed these websites to ensure that they are suitable for students. Many websites change frequently, however, and we cannot guarantee that a site's future contents will continue to meet standards of quality and educational value. Students should be closely supervised whenever they access the Internet.

INDEX

age of the universe 12, 16, 60
alien life 46, 53
amyotrophic lateral sclerosis (ALS) 9, 11, 24, 26, 34, 36, 44–45, 48

Big Bang 12, 18–19, 22, 24, 25, 26, 27, 28, 29
Big Bang Theory, The 49, 50, 54
black holes 4, 12, 14, 20, 22, 24, 25, 37, 39, 55, 60, 61
Bohr, Niels 58
Boyle, Robert 58

Cambridge University 9, 11, 26, 48
computers 8, 31, 35, 49, 54
Copernicus, Nicolaus 15
cosmic background radiation 18, 19, 27

dark energy 52, 59, 61
dark matter 19, 20, 52, 59, 61

earth-centered universe 15
Einstein, Albert 4, 7, 14, 17, 24, 25, 27, 32, 47, 54
elementary particles 32, 38, 39, 61
European Organization for Nuclear Research (CERN) 38, 55, 59
exoplanets 47
expansion of the universe 12, 16–17, 18–19, 26–27, 37, 41, 52, 59

Feynman, Richard P. 30

galaxies 17, 19, 20, 22, 59, 60, 61
Galilei, Galileo 6, 15, 28
Gehrig, Lou 11
gravity 4, 12, 14, 16, 19, 24, 32, 52, 59, 61
Guth, Alan 26, 31

Hartle, James B. 29, 30
Hawking, Elaine (wife) 37, 49
Hawking, Frank (father) 4, 5, 6
Hawking, Isobel Eileen Walker (mother) 4, 6
Hawking, Lucy (daughter) 36, 39, 42, 49
Hawking radiation 22, 23, 24, 39
Hawking, Robert (son) 24, 36, 49
Hawking's works 40–41
  A Brief History of Time 4, 32, 34–35, 36, 37, 39, 40, 54
  "A Smooth Exit from Eternal Inflation?" 41, 48
  George's Secret Key to the Universe 39, 41
  Grand Design, The 41, 48
Hawking, Timothy (son) 36, 49
Higgs boson 38, 39
Hoyle, Fred 11, 15, 16, 19, 24
Hubble, Edwin 17, 20

Laflamme, Raymond 29, 31
Lemaître, Georges 18

Milky Way 17, 20, 60
multiple universes 27, 41

National Aeronautical and Space Administration (NASA) 21, 27, 36, 56
Newton, Sir Isaac 7, 14, 25, 26, 32

Obama, President Barack 42, 49
Oxford University 6, 9, 10–11

particle accelerators 38, 39, 54, 55
Penrose, Sir Roger 24, 25, 31

Relativity, General Theory of 4, 14, 24, 25, 27, 47, 54
rowing club 10
Rubin, Vera 19

school days 7, 8
Sciama, Dennis 11
Simpsons, The 50, 54
singularities 18, 22, 24, 25, 27
space-time 14, 25, 31, 32, 40
space travel 21, 47, 56–57
speech synthesizer 4, 35, 44
stars 12, 16
subatomic particles 14, 30, 38, 39, 52, 54, 55, 58

Tahta, Dikran 7, 8
telescopes 12, 17, 28, 54, 56
Theory of Everything, The 51
time 4, 12, 14, 22, 24, 28, 29, 47
time travel 29, 47

Wilde, Jane 24, 36, 37, 49, 51